DISCOVER DOGS WITH THE AMERICAN CANINE ASSOCIATION

# I LIKE SHIH TZU!

Linda Bozzo

It is the mission of the American Canine Association (ACA) to provide registered dog owners with the educational support needed for raising, training, showing, and breeding the healthiest pets expected by responsible pet owners throughout the world. Through our activities and services, we encourage and support the dog world in order to promote best-known husbandry standards as well as to ensure that the voice and needs of our customers are quickly and properly addressed.

Our continued support, commitment, and direction are guided by our customers, including veterinary, legal, and legislative advisors. ACA aims to provide the most efficient, cooperative, and courteous service to our customers and strives to set the standard for education and problem solving for all who depend on our services.

For more information, please visit www.acacanines.com, email customerservice@acadogs.com, phone 1-800-651-8332, or write to the American Canine Association at PO Box 121107, Clermont, FL 34712.

Published in 2019 by Enslow Publishing, LLC.
101 W. 23rd Street, Suite 240, New York, NY 10011



**Library of Congress Cataloging-in-Publication Data**
Names: Bozzo, Linda, author.
Title: I like Shih tzu! / Linda Bozzo.
Description: New York, NY : Enslow Publishing, 2019. | Series: Discover dogs with the American Canine Association | Includes bibliographical references and index. | Audience: Grades K to 3.
Identifiers: LCCN 2017044743| ISBN 9780766096837 (library bound) | ISBN 9780766096844 (pbk.) | ISBN 9780766096851 (6 pack)
Subjects: LCSH: Shih tzu—Juvenile literature.
Classification: LCC SF429.S64 B69 2017 | DDC 636.76—dc23
LC record available at https://lccn.loc.gov/2017044743

Printed in the United States of America

**To Our Readers:** We have done our best to make sure all websites in this book were active and appropriate when we went to press. However, the author and the publisher have no control over and assume no liability for the material available on those websites or on any websites they may link to. Any comments or suggestions can be sent by email to customerservice@enslow.com.

**Photo Credits:** Cover, p. 1 Eric Isselee/Shutterstock.com; p. 3 (left) Daz Stock/Shutterstock.com; p. 3 (right) Pattarit S/Shutterstock.com; p. 5 Dave King/Dorling Kindersley/Getty Images; p. 6 Nagel Photography/Shutterstock.com; p. 9 A3pfamily/Shutterstock.com; p. 10 © iStockphoto.com/pjgs; p. 13 (puppy) chaoss/Shutterstock.com; p. 13 (collar) graphicphoto/iStock/Thinkstock, (bed) Luisa Leal Photography/Shutterstock.com, (brush) In-Finity/Shutterstock.com, (food and water bowls) exopixel/Shutterstock.com, (leash, toys) © iStockphoto.com/Liliboas; pp. 14, 18 135pixels/Shutterstock.com; p. 17 Luis Marcelo Zanlucki/Moment Open/Getty Images; p. 19 © iStockphoto.com/ProArtWork; p. 21 WilleeCole Photography/Shutterstock.com.

Enslow Publishing
101 W. 23rd Street
Suite 240
New York, NY 10011
USA
enslow.com

# CONTENTS

# IS A SHIH TZU RIGHT FOR YOU?

Shih tzu *(sheed zoo)* are sweet, friendly lapdogs. If you own other small pets, a shih tzu might be right for you.

Many shih tzu are called "shih tzu" or "shih tzus."

# A DOG OR A PUPPY?

Yummy treats make training your shih tzu easier. But training takes time. If you do not have time to train a puppy, you may want an older shih tzu instead.

This small breed needs to learn rules so he doesn't get bossy.

# LOVING YOUR SHIH TZU

Love your shih tzu by spending time with him. He is a cuddly and playful little dog who wants to be around you. Don't be surprised if he follows you everywhere!

Many dog breeds have special jobs they were born to do. But the shih tzu was bred to be a house pet.

## EXERCISE

Shih tzu enjoy short walks on a leash. Indoor games such as fetch will keep your shih tzu healthy and happy.

Shih tzu make great house pets for all ages.

# FEEDING YOUR SHIH TZU

Shih tzu can be fed wet or dry dog food. Ask a veterinarian (vet), a doctor for animals, which food is best for your dog and how much to feed her.

Give your shih tzu fresh, clean water every day.

Remember to keep your dog's food and water dishes clean. Dirty dishes can make a dog sick.

Do not feed your dog people food. It can make her sick.

Your new dog will need:

a collar with a tag

a bed

a brush

food and water dishes

a leash

toys

Shih tzu should be professionally groomed when needed.

# GROOMING

Shih tzu shed very little. This means their hair does not fall out much. Your shih tzu will need to be brushed and combed often. Bathe him as needed. Make sure to use shampoo made specially for dogs.

A shih tzu's nails will need to be clipped. A vet or groomer can show you how. Your dog's ears should be cleaned, and his teeth should be brushed by an adult.

## WHAT YOU SHOULD KNOW

Shih tzu do not bark much. However, they will let you know when they hear or see something.

Because of their short snouts, shih tzus may have breathing problems. Some snore.

Shih tzu do not do well in heat. Keep your shih tzu cool during hot summer days.

You will need to take your new dog to the vet for a checkup. He will need shots, called **vaccinations**, and yearly checkups to keep him healthy. If you think your dog may be sick or hurt, call your vet.

# A GOOD FRIEND

The shih tzu makes a great friend. On your lap or playing games, her big round eyes will warm your heart.

Shih tzu live around 10 to 16 years.

# NOTE TO PARENTS

It is important to consider having your dog spayed or neutered when the dog is young. Spaying and neutering are operations that prevent unwanted puppies and can help improve the overall health of your dog.

It is also a good idea to microchip your dog, in case he or she gets lost. A vet will implant a microchip under the skin containing an identification number that can be scanned at a vet's office or animal shelter. The microchip registry is contacted, and the company uses the ID number to look up your information from a database.

Some towns require licenses for dogs, so be sure to check with your town clerk.

For more information, speak with a vet.

There are many dogs, young and old, waiting to be adopted from animal shelters and rescue groups.

## Words to Know

**fetch** To go after a toy and bring it back.

**groomer** A person who bathes and brushes dogs.

**leash** A chain or strap that attaches to a dog's collar.

**shed** When dog hair falls out so new hair can grow.

**vaccinations** Shots that dogs need to stay healthy.

**veterinarian (vet)** A doctor for animals.

# Read About Dogs

## Books

Gray, Susan Heinrichs. *Shih Tzus*. New York, NY: AV2 by Weigl, 2016

Morey, Allan. *Shih Tzus*. North Mankato, MN: Capstone Press, 2017.

Schuetz, Kari. *Shih Tzus*. Jefferson City, MO: Scholastic, 2017.

## Websites

**American Canine Association Inc., Kids Corner**
*www.acakids.com*
Visit the official website of the American Canine Association.

**National Geographic for Kids, Pet Central**
*kids.nationalgeographic.com/explore/pet-central/*
Learn more about dogs and other pets at the official site of the National Geographic Society for Kids.

# INDEX